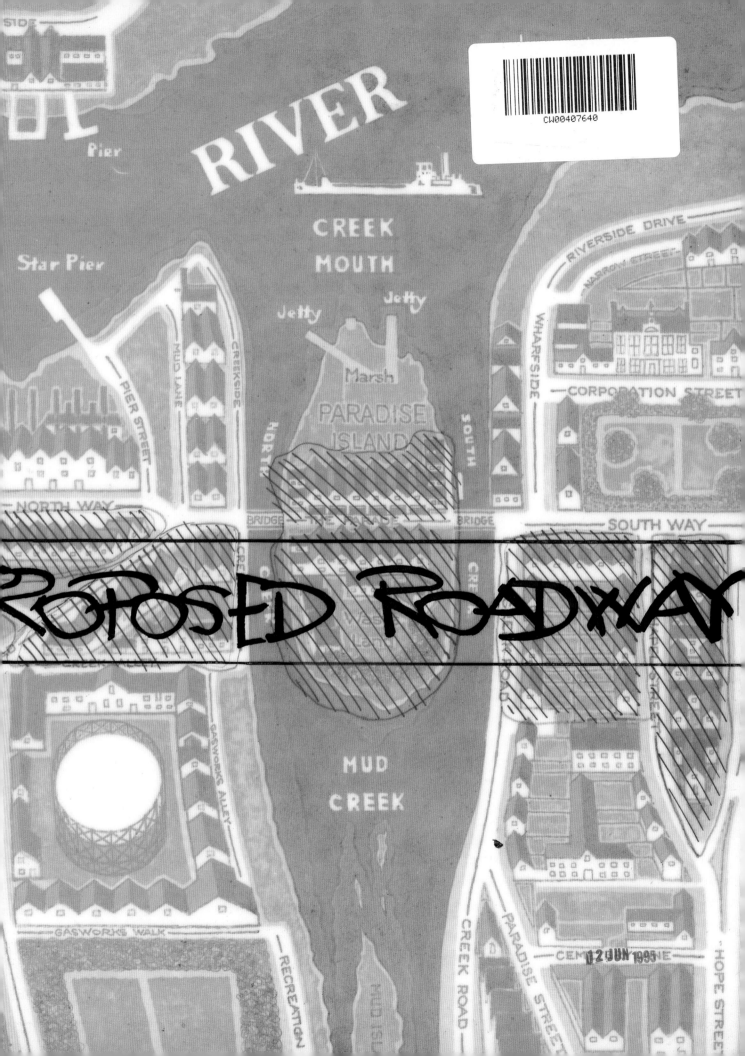

RIVER

CREEK
MOUTH

Star Pier

Pier

Jetty

Jetty

Marsh

PARADISE
ISLAND

RIVERSIDE DRIVE

NARROW STREET

WHARFSIDE

CORPORATION STREET

NORTH

SOUTH

MUD LANE

CREEKSIDE

PIER STREET

NORTH WAY

BRIDGE

THE HOUSE

BRIDGE

SOUTH WAY

PROPOSED ROADWAY

West Mead

MUD
CREEK

GASWORKS ALLEY

GASWORKS WALK

RECREATION

MUD ISL

CREEK ROAD

PARADISE STREET

CEMETERY

HOPE STREET

12 JUN 1995

Tid - environmental

Tid - environmental

CHARLES KEEPING

ADAM

AND

Paradise Island

SAVE OUR ISLAND — NO TO MOTORWAY

Oxford University Press

OXFORD · NEW YORK · TORONTO

Down the river, past the warehouses and factories, was a muddy creek with a small island in the middle. The local people called it Paradise Isle. It wasn't much of a place, but to Adam it was home and he was happy there.

Little stone bridges connected it to either side of the creek, and a narrow roadway, called The Parade, ran across the centre. Traffic travelling north or south had to use the roadway or add miles to their journey.

A few old shops and warehouses lined The Parade, and through the window of The Island Bookshop you could survey the whole scene.

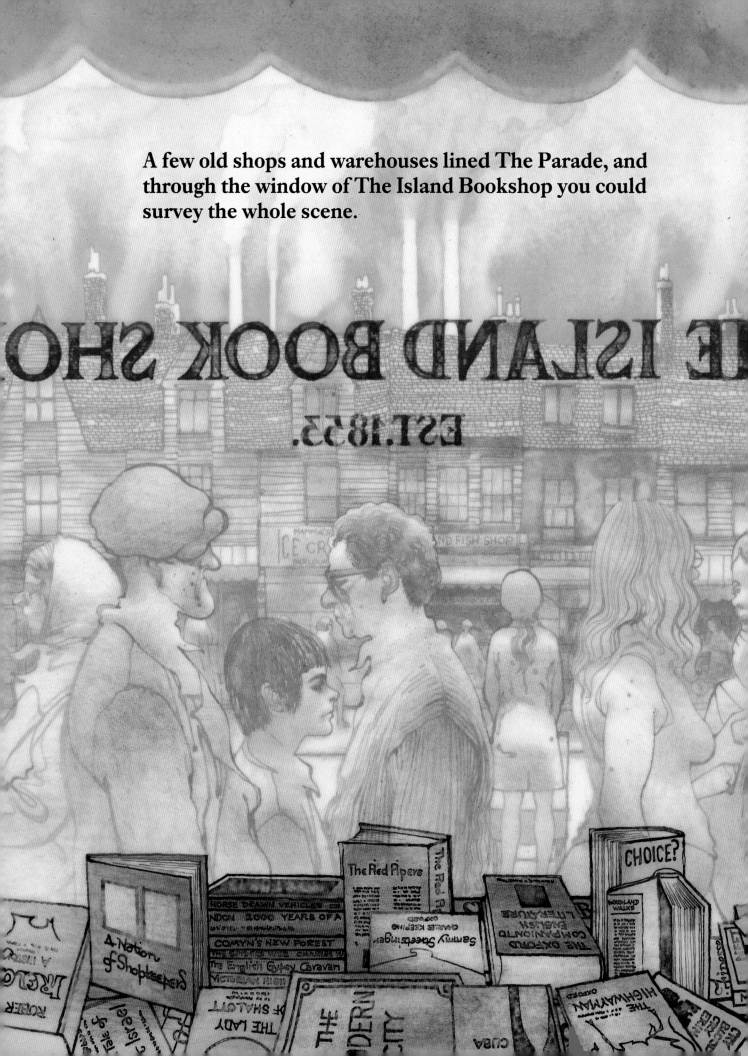

You could find Sarah Sprout, happy among her fruit and vegetables, or Bertie Bull standing outside his butcher's shop.

There was Percy Pike making patterns of fish on the marble slabs, and Betty Bun, smiling sweetly behind her cakes, breads, and pastries.

Adam was friendly with them all, but his favourite place was an overgrown marshy patch where Old Varda lived with his caravan, pony and cart, goat and chickens. Long ago he'd been a travelling man but now he just passed his time whittling driftwood, washed up on the foreshore, into little toys.

On the other side of the marsh was a dilapidated pier with an old painted barge moored alongside. This was the home of Ma Burley, retired now from a life on the river and canals,

her sole companions an old shaggy dog and two singing birds in a cage. Like most old people, they liked to tell the young folk of their travels and adventures in days passed.

Across on the mainland the local councillors met weekly to discuss the affairs of the borough. They loved planning and couldn't stand what they thought was chaos. To them Paradise Island was just a wasteful mess. But they couldn't think what to do with it. Many ideas were suggested, from a heliport to a rubbish tip. Finally they got it!

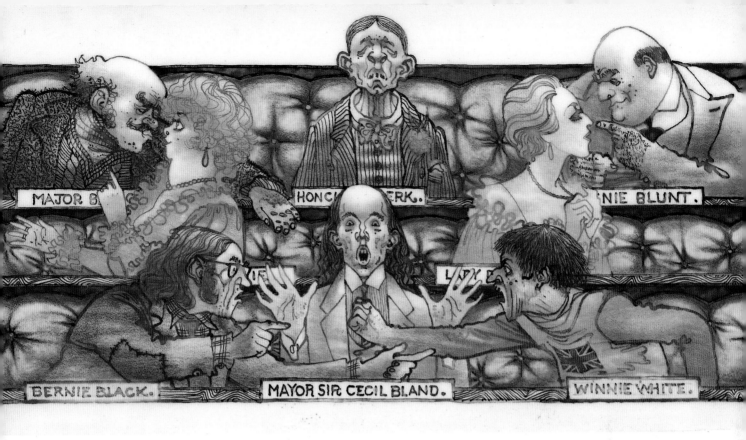

At their next meeting, they decided to build a fast toll road across the island, linking either side of the creek. This would improve traffic flow north and south and put lots of money into the coffers. (Bernie and Winnie abstained as usual.)

Once this plan was finalized, they quickly passed a compulsory purchase order on the old shops and warehouses. And then the bulldozers moved in

to knock them flat. The shopkeepers were all promised
new homes on the mainland.

Weeks later, Adam came to see his old friends on the marsh.
He was dismayed at all the destruction, until Ma Burley
told him that fortunately their patch was no good for building
and was to be walled off and left to nature.

It was then that Old Varda let him in on a brilliant idea
they'd had. Adam was thrilled when he heard it and
dashed off, soon to return with a small army
of his friends.

Together, they began collecting lots of the discarded timber
and bricks from the demolition site.

They loaded it all on to Old Varda's cart to
transport it down to the marsh.

Later, as the building of the new roadway progressed, fresh white concrete appeared where the old shops and warehouses had been. The councillors watched with pride.

They admired their power to alter the landscape of the island so completely.

Meanwhile, on the marsh things were also taking shape. New structures began to appear.

Even the councillors approved of this work because it
silenced their critics and also made them look benevolent.

Time passed by and finally the new road was finished,
spanning the island like some gigantic spider.
On their big day, the councillors, except of course
Bernie and Winnie, surveyed their creation with pride.

Then, at the appointed time, Gerry Bandynose, a current
TV and radio idol, was invited to cut the tape and
declare the road officially open.

Unfortunately, once the tape was cut, the councillors found themselves completely ignored by the vast crowds who had arrived mainly to see Gerry Bandynose.

Mounted policemen were needed to control the adoring girls, rival gangs of hooligans, and various demonstrators who had all turned up.

You see, none of the local people were the slightest bit interested in the roadway. Only the drivers of cars and lorries, speeding north or south found it useful, and most of them were completely unaware of the island's existence.

They were too busy watching the road and listening to Gerry Bandynose on their radios.

Now that their old shops were gone, the shopkeepers all got new jobs in the freezer department of the new Neata Supermarket.

And in the evening they all went home to their Neata homes nearby.

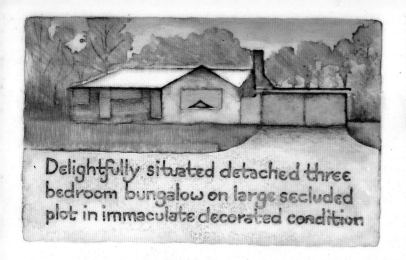

Delightfully situated detached three bedroom bungalow on large secluded plot in immaculate decorated condition.

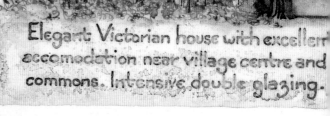

Elegant Victorian house with excellent accomodation near village centre and commons. Intensive double glazing.

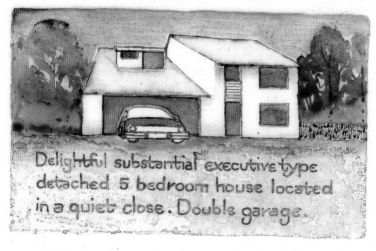

Delightful substantial executive type detached 5 bedroom house located in a quiet close. Double garage.

Right on top of the woodlands. A quite outstanding residence with 4 bedrooms. Beautifully decorated.

5 bedroom detached house in highly sought after residential quiet road overlooking golf course. Desirable.

Quite unique house. Polished oak strip flooring throughout. Master bedroom en-suite with jacuzzi. Superb condition

5 bedroom Tudor style detached house behind brick wall and wrought-iron security gates. Panoramic veiws.

Character detached bungalow in a ½ acre, in quiet cul de sac. Close to a open heath and station. 3 bedroom.

The councillors were of course disappointed by the disarray of the opening ceremony, but, nevertheless, with a feeling of satisfaction at a job well done, they went back to their detached homes in the leafy suburbs further down the river.

Behind the wall on the marsh, Ma Burley and Old Varda, who had been appointed as official guardians of the playground, were happily cooking sausages and baked potatoes.

So in the end everyone got something out of the island project: the councillors felt they'd done a great service for the borough, the shopkeepers got new jobs and homes, the road-users a nice flat throughway, the children a playground, and Ma Burley and Old Varda the chance to do a useful job in their old age.

Paradise Isle eventually meant something different to all concerned, that is, of course with the exception of Bernie and Winnie, which only goes to show that you can never quite please everyone.

CHARLES KEEPING
1924–1988

Charles Keeping illustrated and wrote books for
Oxford University Press for over 30 years. He
was widely recognized as one of the most
brilliant and original artists of his generation.
He died on 16 May 1988. This was his last book
for us.

Oxford University Press, Walton Street, Oxford OX2 6DP
Oxford New York Toronto
Delhi Bombay Calcutta Madras Karachi
Petaling Jaya Singapore Hong Kong Tokyo
Nairobi Dar es Salaam Cape Town
Melbourne Auckland

and associated companies in
Berlin Ibadan

Oxford is a trade mark of Oxford University Press

Copyright © Charles Keeping 1989

First published in the UK by Oxford University Press 1989
Reprinted 1989, 1990

British Library Cataloguing in Publication Data

Keeping, Charles, 1924-88
Adam and Paradise Island
I. Title
823'.914[J]
ISBN 0 19 279842 1

Typeset by PGT Design, Oxford
Printed in Hong Kong

Roadway Across Paradise Island.

For:

Mayor Bleince DFE HJS

Hon Chauub Berk

Ernie Blunt

Sybil Sillis

Lady Primrose Smith

Samuel Bland XYZ.

Against:

Bernie Black

Minnie White

Borough Clerk:

Ivor Abel Penn

Witness:

Saul Mark Dunn